Tigger's Family Tree

Disney's

A Winnie the Pooh First Reader

Tigger's Family Tree

by Isabel Gaines

ILLUSTRATED BY Studio Orlando

Disney PRESS

NEW YORK

Tigger's Family Tree

One crisp fall day,
Tigger asked all his friends
to go bouncing with him.

But nobody would.

Poor Tigger

felt very lonely.

Roo tried to cheer up Tigger.

"I have a mother," said Roo.

"Maybe you have a family, too."

"Hey, that would be great!"

said Tigger.

"But I don't know where
they live," Tigger said.

"Maybe Owl can help," Roo said.

So off they went to Owl's house.

"To find one's family," said Owl,
"one must first look up
one's family tree."

Tigger and Roo

searched and searched

for Tigger's family tree.

"Yoo-hoo! Family tree!"

Tigger shouted.

Finally, they gave up

and went back to Tigger's house.

Tigger sat at his desk.

Roo sat on Tigger's desk

beside a pile of letters.

"Oh, where are those tiggers,

anyway?" said Tigger.

"We've looked everywhere."

15

Roo picked up a letter.

"Maybe there's another way

to find them," said Roo.

"I'll write them a letter!"

said Tigger.

"Dear T-I–double Guh–Rrrs, Tiggers.

Greetings. Please drop by

any old time.

Love, Tigger."

They put the letter
in the mailbox.

"Now there's nothing to do
but wait," Tigger said.

18

Tigger and Roo waited.

And they waited.

After a while,

it started to snow.

Finally Tigger said,

"I might as well face it,

there aren't any other tiggers."

Tigger sadly went back inside.

Roo wanted to make Tigger

feel better.

He decided Tigger's friends

should write a pretend letter

to Tigger from his family.

Owl wrote, "Dear Tigger,

Just a note to say—"

"Dress warmly," said Kanga.

"Eat well," said Pooh.

"Stay safe and sound,"

said Piglet.

"Keep smiling," said Eeyore.

"We're always there for you,"

said Roo.

"Wishing you all the best,

signed, your family," finished Owl.

"I got a letter from my family,"
Tigger said the next morning.
"They are coming to visit.
Tomorrow."

Tigger bounced off
to get ready.

"Oh, dear," said Kanga.

"He'll be so sad

when they don't arrive."

But Roo had another idea.

"My family!" said Tigger.

"I'm so happy

to meet you all!"

"Roo?" Tigger asked.

"Why are you dressed like a tigger?

Piglet, Owl, Kanga, and Eeyore!

You're NOT my family!"

Tigger left the party.

He went back into the woods

to find his family tree.

He came to a tree

covered with stripes!

But Tigger could not find

any tiggers in the tree.

It wasn't a tigger family tree

after all.

"Tigger?" Roo said,

coming up behind him.

"Are you okay?"

Tigger looked at Roo
and all his friends.
"Maybe you ARE
my family,"
said Tigger.

31

"Of course we are,"

said Christopher Robin.

Christopher Robin

took a picture of Tigger

and his friends.

"It's my family picture!"
said Tigger happily.

Can you match the words with the

pictures?

letter

Tigger

family

mailbox

bouncing

Fill in the missing letters.

R_o

mot_er

t_ee

pi_ture

s_ow

Follow all the adventures
of Pooh and his friends!